Kevin and the Seven Lions

by

Martin Tiller

Illustrated by Carla Tracy

DEDICATION

To all my teachers that were frustrated with my daydreaming.

To my own students, never lose your imagination.

ACKNOWLEDGMENTS

Thank you to my parents. Thank you to all of my teachers. Thank you to my wife, Heather, for reading and supporting a very early version of this book, and for putting up with all the playing on the computer, from which this book was born.

To Rachel, for making a growling noise at the dinosaur when you first saw this book.

Thank you to Carla Tracy for the breathtaking illustrations, without which Kevin would not exist.

Kevin was being chased by dinosaurs. He was in a hurry.

His heart pounded.

It hurt inside his chest.

He felt the dinosaur's breath on his neck.

"Kevin I need your attention," said Mrs. Calvin.

"Kevin!" Mrs. Calvin spoke louder.

He looked around and didn't see any dinosaurs, he only saw his class.

Kevin went to Holly Hills Elementary School, and he was in the third grade.

Mrs. Calvin was his teacher.

"Kevin, thank you for giving me your attention, how many baseballs does a team have if three boys bring three baseballs each?"

"Nine" said Kevin.

"Thank you, Kevin."

Kevin was sad to not be chased by dinosaurs.

Math practice isn't as exciting. His heart raced, but it just isn't the same.

Kevin started his work, and he tried not to daydream the rest of the day.

The submarine was quiet. The lights from the ceiling were the only source of light. Kevin looked out the window. He squinted.

He saw the first tentacle, then the second, and then another. They were huge, and they were getting closer. Then a gigantic eye filled up the window!

7

"Kevin, I need you to finish your writing. Thank you."

Kevin began writing about what he did over the weekend. He wished he had been in an actual submarine. Writing about cutting the grass didn't hold the same interest.

Kevin liked third grade. But where he went in his head was far better.

Kevin exhausted Mrs. Calvin from time to time, but she did her best to keep him focused.

Kevin put his pencil down. He put his hands in front of him and looked at the wall.

The spaceship came out of light speed, and the sandy red planet floated in front of him. Three fighters came into view from the left side. They did not seem to be friendly. They looked like three flying bats. Red lights flashed all around him. Sirens blared throughout the ship.

"Kevin get back to work," said Mrs. Calvin from her desk where she was reading with other students.

Kevin felt embarrassed, and the spaceship was nowhere to be found.

Disappointed he picked his pencil up and got back to work.

He was beginning to wish he didn't daydream so much.

Mrs. Calvin noticed his embarrassment, and a thought popped into her head.

"Kevin I want to know what you are thinking about when you daydream," she asked him later in the day.

"Um...Okay." Kevin wanted this conversation to end. Mrs. Calvin would never want to know about spaceships and dinosaurs.

"I want you to start writing down what you see when you daydream."

"Um...Okay." This was weird.

"Promise me you will try this. I am giving you a clean notebook to just write down what you daydream."

"When am I supposed to write in this?"

"Take it home. Write down what you daydream during class. Write down the whole daydream I want to see what happens."

Kevin wasn't sure what to think. Was this a trick? Was he going to be graded on this? Is this going to be shown to his parents?

When Kevin got home he threw his backpack into the corner of his room.

He never thought about the notebook.

The next day Kevin came to school. The notebook was still in his backpack.

He found it, when he pulled out his class binder. He quietly put the notebook in his desk, and Tuesday began normally.

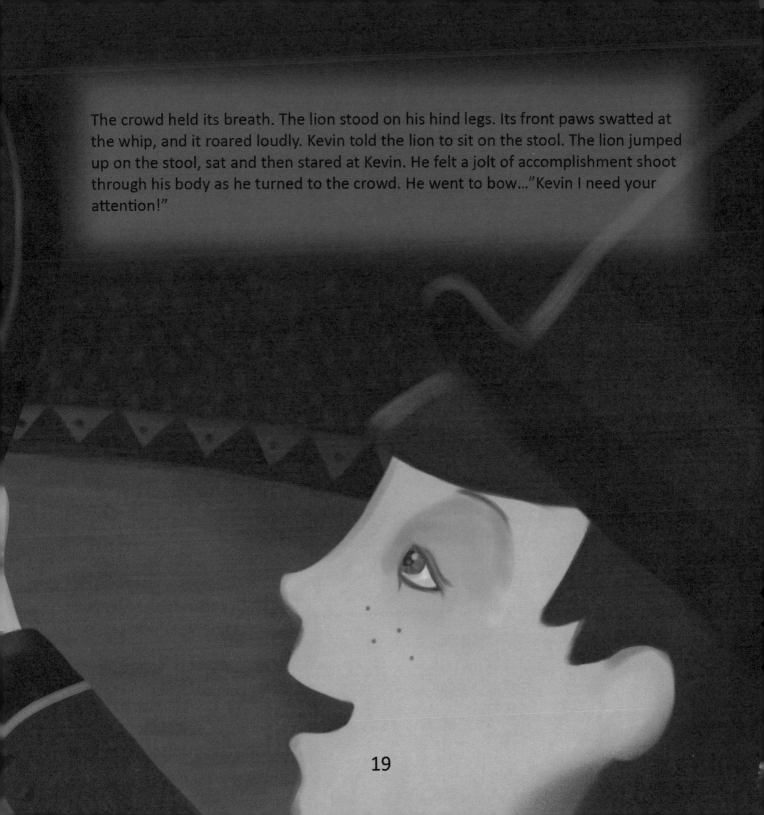

The crowd held its breath. The lion stood on his hind legs. Its front paws swatted at the whip, and it roared loudly. Kevin told the lion to sit on the stool. The lion jumped up on the stool, sat and then stared at Kevin. He felt a jolt of accomplishment shoot through his body as he turned to the crowd. He went to bow..."Kevin I need your attention!"

19

He came back to the real world.

Mrs. Calvin looked at Kevin and realized that Kevin should write down his daydream at that moment.

"Kevin, take three minutes and write."

"Write what?"

"Kevin," Mrs. Calvin shot him a look.

He got out his notebook. He took three minutes to write about being a lion tamer that had seven lions in his show.

After three minutes was up, he closed his book, and went back to sorting simple machines for his science assignment.

21

That bus ride home was different. He didn't speak to anyone. He was busy being a lion tamer. Seven lions surrounded him inside a black metal cage. Flashbulbs went off behind the lions as the crowd took pictures of the Magnificent Kevin and His Lions.

His friends had to remind him to get off the bus to go home.

When he got home he walked right past his mom, and his little brother who was playing video games. His mom was worried. Kevin always stopped and played video games with Michael.

"How was your day?" she asked.

Kevin responded "It was fine," and he continued to his room.

Kevin opened the door to his room and sat down at his desk. He opened his backpack and pulled out the notebook that Mrs. Calvin gave him.

Kevin sharpened a pencil.
He began writing.

"Six lions walked into the center ring cage. "
He continued writing until his mom came to his door to call him down to dinner. Kevin was still at his desk writing. His mom was a little confused about this behavior, no video games, no TV, what was going on with Kevin?

At dinner his dad asked him how his day was.

"Fine," Kevin responded.

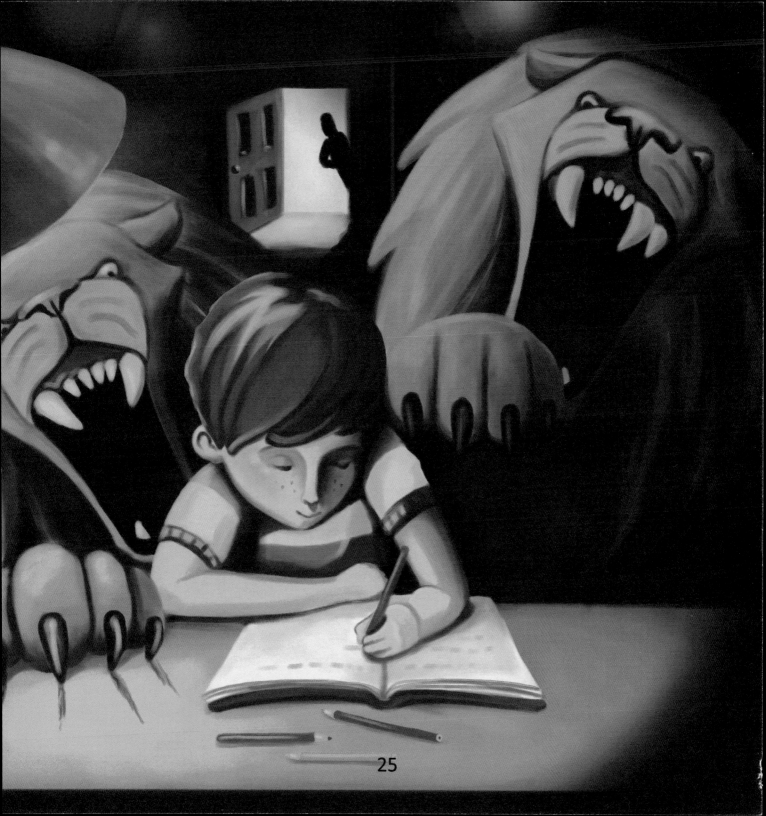

After dinner Kevin went back upstairs and continued writing about Kevin the Magnificent and the Seven Lions.

An hour later his mom and dad stood at Kevin's door and stared at what they saw.

Kevin was sitting still at his desk writing.

They wondered. Was he in trouble? Does he have a lot of extra homework? Was he sick?

"Kevin, what are you doing?" his dad asked.
Kevin put down his pencil.

"I'm writing."

"Is it your homework?"

"In a way, Mrs. Calvin asked me to write down my daydreams, she said she wants to read about where I go when I stop paying attention."

"That's very interesting!" Said Kevin's dad. "Can I hear about your daydream?"

"Um, okay." Kevin was nervous, was he going to be in trouble?

He started reading about Kevin the Magnificent and the Seven Lions.

"Kevin the Magnificent walked into the center ring cage. The crowd clapped loudly. He took a deep bow, and then he snapped his whip in the air. The crowd clapped louder."

Kevin kept reading. His parents listened quietly.

"Six lions walked into the center ring cage. Kevin the Magnificent held up his whip and shouted a command. All the lions sat down.

He then shouted another command, and all six lions stood up on their hind legs. The crowd cheered loudly. And then he cracked his whip and all the lions sat back down.

Kevin the Magnificent knew the show was going great.

Then Leo the Lion entered the ring. Leo was a very big lion. He was scary big. All the other lions sat quietly, when Leo entered the ring. Leo let out a loud roar. It hurt Kevin's ears. Leo lunged at Kevin. The audience gasped.

Kevin took several steps backwards. He held his whip high. Kevin shouted a command and cracked the whip. Leo took a step back and roared even louder than before. One more time, Kevin shouted a command and cracked his whip. Leo took another step back, and then jumped up on a stool and sat down.

The audience cheered. Kevin shouted another command and cracked his whip, and all seven lions stood up on their hind legs. The audience stood on their feet cheering loudly. Kevin gave one last command, and all the lions walked in a line out of the Center Ring. The audience roared loudly. Kevin took a big bow, and then he followed his lions out of the ring."

33

Kevin put down his story. He had finished it.

"Kevin! That was a great story! The lions were great, especially the big scary one at the end! Have you written any other stories?"

"Ah, no," Kevin was confused he spent a lot of his time being in trouble for the things that he did. This was different.

"Well, if you ever write another story I would love to read it! Maybe you can dream about your next story tonight when you sleep. You should keep that notebook next to your bed, and if you have a dream write it down."

Kevin actually liked that idea. He got ready for bed.

As he climbed into bed, he shut the notebook, and placed a pencil on top of it. He stared at the notebook thinking about the next story that he would write in it.

He closed his eyes.

He was so happy that his mom and dad liked his story about Kevin the Magnificent and the Seven Lions. That was a great feeling.

What else would his mom and dad like to read about?

Kevin walked to his fighter jet. He climbed in and started up the engines. He then flew off into the bright blue sky.

Kevin then went to sleep, and he dreamed.

He got up the next morning and began to write.

39

ABOUT THE AUTHOR

Martin Tiller currently teaches first grade in Virginia, where he lives with his wife Heather, daughter Rachel, and his Star Wars named cats, Kamino and Naboo, and dog, Leia.

ABOUT THE ILLUSTRATOR

Carla Tracy is a UK based Designer and Illustrator, who was apparently born with a pencil in her hand, and loves nothing more than to get creative. Her first notable artistic endeavour was at Primary school, where she sculpted an entire family of Hedgehogs out of clay. She currently lives on a solitary old farm in rural Leicestershire, with her spirited little Sausage Dog as a sidekick.

You can find Kevin at Facebook.com/KevinAndTheSevenLions

Martin Tiller can be found at amazon.com/author/martin_tiller

Carla Tracy can be found at Facebook.com/CarlaTracyIllustration